Martha Go, Go, Goes Green!

Adaptation by Karen Barss
Based on a TV series teleplay written by Ron Holsey
Based on the characters created by Susan Meddaugh

HOUGHTON MIFFLIN HARCOURT
Boston • New York • 2013

AGES	GRADES	GUIDED READING LEVEL	READING RECOVERY LEVEL	LEXILE® LEVEL
6–8	2/3	L	19	480L

For information about permission to reproduce selections from this book, write to Permissions, Houghton Mifflin Harcourt, 215 Park Avenue South, New York, New York 10003.

Library of Congress Cataloging-in-Publication Data is on file.

ISBN: 978-0-547-99547-2 hardcover
ISBN: 978-0-547-97017-2 paperback

Design by Rachel Newborn

www.hmhbooks.com
www.marthathetalkingdog.com

Manufactured in China
SCP 10 9 8 7 6 5 4 3 2 1
4500387120

"There is going to be a go-cart race next week!" says Helen.
"It's called the Go Green Go-Cart Race."
"Will you enter with me?" Helen asks.

"Your cart has to be green?" asks Martha. "'Green' means you have to use alternative energy to fuel your cart," says Helen.

"Alternative energy is energy that's different from gas or oil," says Helen.
"Using energy from the sun or the wind is better for the planet."

But how does it work?

Helen and Martha do some research.
"Solar cells change sunlight into electricity.
Dad could get us some solar cells!" says
Helen.

Helen draws what the cart will look like.
"Now all we need is some parts," she says.
"Let's go to the junkyard," says Martha.

T.D. and Alice are at the junkyard too.
"Are you entering the go-cart race?" asks Helen.
"Yes," says T.D. "So are Ronald and Reginald."

"What kind of cart are you making?"
asks Helen.
"We are making a wind-powered cart,"
says T.D.
"Wind creates a lot of clean energy."

Dad helps Helen and Martha build a cart using solar cells and parts from the junkyard.

Finally, the big day arrives!
Everyone lines up at the starting line.
And they are off!

But a giant cloud covers the sun.
There is no solar energy to power
Martha and Helen's cart!

T.D. and Alice are still at the starting line too.
There is no wind.

Ronald and Reginald are in the lead.
What kind of energy are they using?

Just then the sun comes out.
Martha and Helen begin to move!
A strong gust of wind whips down the street.
Alice and T.D. are finally in the race!

T.D. and Alice fly from last place to second!
It is a close race.
But, they finish right behind Ronald and
Reginald.

"Congratulations," says Junkyard Joe.
"Tell us how your cart works."

"When the fish swims, it generates energy," explains Ronald.
"Really?" says Junkyard Joe.
"Can we see your cart in action one last time?"

Both boys want to drive.
They fight and crash into a post.

The cart breaks open.
It is a lawnmower!

"Gasoline is not alternative energy," says
Martha.
"T.D. and Alice are the *real* winners!"

Junkyard Joe gives the trophy to
Alice and T.D.
"Now let's take a photo of you and
your cart," he says.
"Say, where is it?"

They look around.
The go-cart is nowhere in sight.

The wind took it all the way to
Dog Head Lake.

Wind energy sure
can be powerful!

Hot Stuff!

Have you ever noticed that if you touch the sidewalk on a summer day, the cement feels hot? The sidewalk has absorbed heat, or solar energy, from the sun.

- *Solar* is the Latin word for sun.

- Some buildings have *solar panels* on the roof to collect heat from the sun to make *energy.* People use windmills (for wind) and dams (for water) to make *power,* just like you use healthy food to power your body!

Go Green!

- Solar, wind, and water power are *renewable.* That means they can be replaced or renewed. They will never run out.

- Renewable energy is also called *green* or clean energy. Renewable energy does not *pollute.* It does not make waste that can get into the air or water and harm living things.